The world's best
JOKES
for kids
VOLUME 2

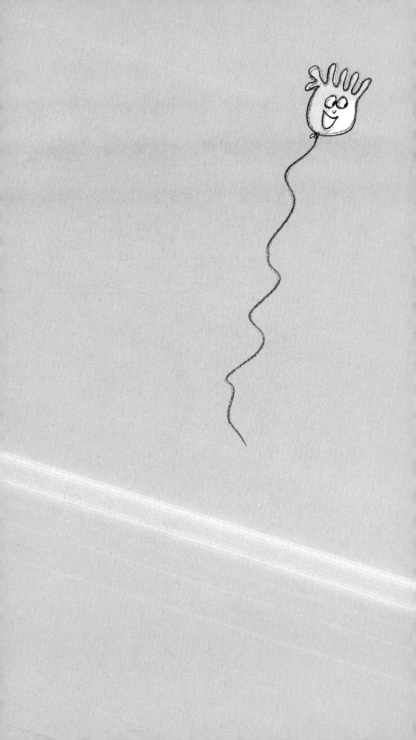

The world's best
JOKES
for kids
VOLUME 2

Every single one
illustrated

SWERLING & LAZAR

Andrews McMeel
PUBLISHING®

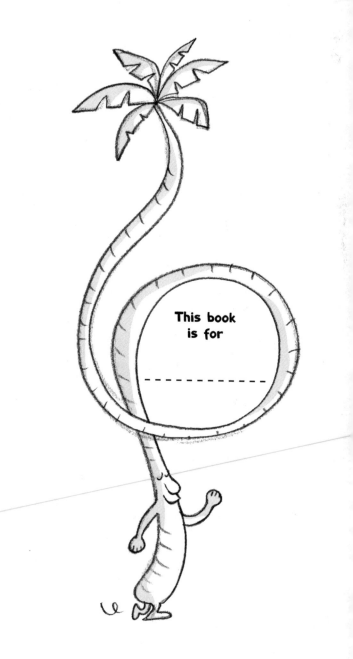

This book
is for

Why is it impossible for a leopard to hide?

Because he will always be spotted.

What can be served but never eaten?

A tennis ball.

What type of dance do plumbers love?

Tap dance.

I was hoping to win the sun-tanning Olympics...

...but I only got bronze.

What do you call a boring dinosaur?

A dino-snore.

When is the best time to go to the dentist?

At tooth hurty.

What do you call a bee having a bad hair day?

A frisbee.

What dogs make the best scientists?

Labs.

What do you call a police cat?

Claw enforcement.

Why is England the wettest country?

Because the Queen has reigned there for years.

Who shaves ten times a day but still has a beard?

A barber.

Why did the banana go to the doctor?

It wasn't peeling well.

What do you get if you eat pasta when you have a cold?

Macaroni sneeze.

7

What fruit
keeps teasing
people?

The ba-na-na-na-na-na.

**When is it best
to buy a chick?**

**When it's
going cheep.**

Why is a bird
more talented
than a fly?

**A bird can fly
but a fly can't bird.**

What lives in the ocean and is good for public transport?

An octobus.

I tried to sue the airport for misplacing my bags.

I lost the case.

Why did the octopus beat the shark in a fight?

Because the octopus was well armed.

How do you make 7 an even number?

Get rid of the S.

Which is the best season for jumping on trampolines?

Spring.

What starts with a T, ends with a T, and is full of T?

A teapot.

Why did the sheep keep going down the road?

There were no ewe-turns allowed.

What did the stamp say to the envelope?

Roger Lightbottom
1001 Crocolide Blvd
Paris
07050, France

"Stick with me and we'll go places."

Where do sharks come from?

Finland.

What's a pirate's favorite hobby?

Ahrrrrt.

What happened when the semi-colon broke the grammar laws?

It was given two consecutive sentences.

Why should you never get into a fight with 1, 3, 5, 7, and 9?

Because the odds will be against you.

What kind of songs do planets sing?

Nep-tunes.

How does a cat get what it wants?

With gentle purr-suasion.

What do you call five giraffes?

A high five.

What do ghosts
use to wash
their hair?

Sham-boo!

Which city never stays
in the same place for long?

Rome.

Why would you put sugar under your pillow?

So that you have sweet dreams.

What is the worst kind of cat to have?

A cat-astrophe.

What did mama cow say to little cow?

"It's pasture bedtime."

What's big, white, and lives on Mars?

A Martian-mallow.

What's the most tired part of a car?

The exhaust pipe.

How do whales cry?

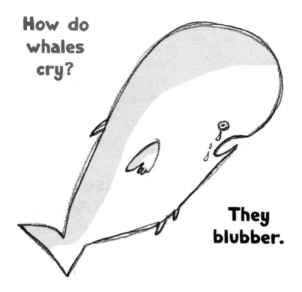

They blubber.

What do you call 2 octopi that look exactly the same?

Itenticle.

Why did the girl eat her homework?

Because her teacher said it was a piece of cake.

Finally they're making a film about clocks.

It's about time.

Have you heard
the joke about
the skunk?

Never mind, it really stinks.

What do you get
when you cross fish
and elephants?

**Swimming
trunks.**

Why didn't the young
pirate go to the movie?

Because it was ahrrr-rated.

What do you call a bee
that's difficult to hear?

A mumble-bee.

Why shouldn't you bring a chicken to school?

It might use fowl language.

Why did the cabinet go to the psychiatrist?

Because it kept talking to its shelf.

What did the one raindrop say to the other?

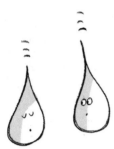

"Two's company, three's a cloud."

What's green and fuzzy and if it fell out of a tree would hurt you?

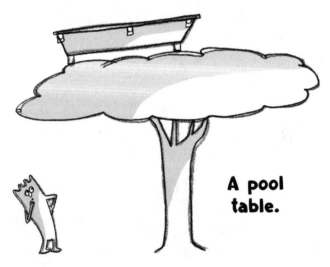

A pool table.

Can a match box?

No, but a tin can.

What do you get from a pampered cow?

Spoiled milk.

Why do pirates take ages to learn the alphabet?

Because they spend years at C.

Why didn't the pig get invited to any parties?

Because he was a boar.

How do you get
a square root?

Plant a tree in
a square pot.

What has four eyes
but can't see?

Mississippi.

How did Dracula
feel when he ate
a sheep?

Baaaaaaaad.

I'm marrying a pencil.

I can't wait to introduce my parents to my bride 2B.

What's black and white and eats like a horse?

A zebra.

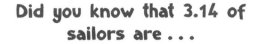

Did you know that 3.14 of sailors are . . .

Pi-rates.

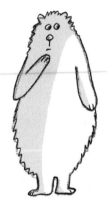

Why didn't the bear go to college?

Because bears don't go to college.

How do trees use their email accounts?

They just log in.

Why do cows have hooves instead of feet?

Because they lactose.

How can you tell if there's an elephant in your sandwich?

It's too heavy to lift.

Where do ghosts go swimming?

Lake Eerie.

What do you call a group of
rabbits walking backwards?

**A receding
hare line.**

Why are mountain ranges funny?

Because they are hill-areas.

WOULD YOU RATHER...

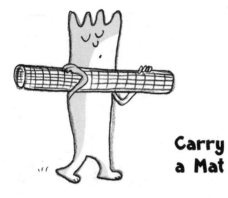

Carry
a Mat

... or Marry
a Cat?

Why are mummies so vain?

Because they're all wrapped up in themselves.

What bread has the worst attitude?

Sour-dough.

How do you make a glass of milkshake?

Give it a fright.

English can be
a complicated
language to
learn.

It can be understood through
tough, thorough thought, though.

What happens when dinosaurs
drive cars too fast?

Tyrannosaurus wrecks.

Why did it take him 4 hours to finish the 20 page book?

Because he wasn't very hungry.

What kind of road do ghosts like?

Dead ends.

**What do you call
a crazy chicken?**

A cuckoo cluck.

**What rock group has four men
that don't sing?**

Mount Rushmore.

Why did the cat put
the letter M into
the freezer?

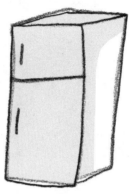

Because it turns ice into Mice.

What did the couch
say while climbing
Everest?

"Sofa, so good."

**What do you get
when you cross a snowman
with a vampire?**

Frosbite.

**What do you call
a napping bull?**

A bulldozer.

**What happens when you
throw a blue pebble
into the Red Sea?**

It gets wet.

Why did the boy tip-toe past the medicine cupboard?

Because he didn't want to wake the sleeping pills.

Which driver will never get a parking ticket?

A screwdriver.

What did the rude triangle say to the circle?

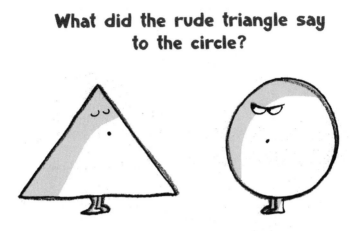

"You're pointless!"

Why was the man fired from the calendar factory?

He took a day off.

Why did the dinosaur cross the road?

Because chickens didn't exist yet.

What wears glass slippers and weighs 8000 pounds?

Cinderelephant.

Why did the octopus blush?

**Because the
sea weed.**

What was wrong with the
wooden car that had wooden
wheels and a wooden engine?

**It wooden
drive.**

What do you say when you throw a clock in the air?

"Time's up!"

How did Benjamin Franklin feel about discovering electricity?

He was totally shocked.

Why did H feel lost and alone?

Because he was in the
middle of nowhere.

What's the
coldest
tropical
island?

Brrrrrrrr-muda.

Why did the invisible man decide not to take the job?

He just couldn't see himself doing it.

What did the table say to the chair?

"Dinner's on me."

What's the capital of California?

C.

What do you call it when a chicken stumbles as it crosses the road.

A road trip.

Why were they worried about the small bucket?

Because it was a little pail.

How do
chickens
dance?

Chick to chick.

**What's a crocodile's
favorite game?**

Snap.

What kind of bow is
impossible to tie?

A rainbow.

What do you call
a dead fly?

A flew.

What kind of crazy
creature lives on
the moon?

A lunar tick.

What happened
to the lost cattle?

Nobody's herd.

Did you hear about
the ant that was very
smart?

**He was
brilli-ant.**

Why did the
bicycle fall
over?

Because it was
two tired.

What do you call a cow who
works for a gardener?

HERB'S
GARDENING
SERVICE

A lawn moo-er.

Why do dogs wag their tails?

Because no one else will do it for them.

What do you get if you put a family of ducks in a carton?

A box of quackers.

What do you call a cat with 8 legs that likes to swim?

An octopuss.

How do ghosts send letters abroad?

Scaremail.

What do you
call a cow in
a tornado?

A milkshake.

Why don't you
ever see hippos
hiding in trees?

Because they're very good at it.

What is white, has four ears, whiskers, and sixteen wheels?

**Two bunnies
on rollerblades.**

**What's a cat's favorite
breakfast?**

Mice Krispies.

What kind of music do balloons hate.

Pop!

Why did the boy eat the candle?

His mother told him to have a light snack.

Why did the girl study on top of the mountain?

She wanted a higher education.

What do aliens put their tea cups on?

Flying saucers.

What did the cat say to the dog?

"Check meow-t!"

If you eat 3/4ths of a pie, what do you get?

A stomachache.

What time is it when an elephant sits on your fence?

Time to get a new fence.

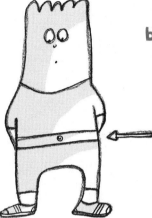

What kind of button can't be undone?

A bellybutton.

What has four legs and one head but only one foot?

A bed.

What type of cheese is made backward?

Edam.

What did the marmalade say to the bread?

"Stop loafing about!"

Why wouldn't the teddy bear eat anything?

He was already stuffed.

Why did the
hamburger lose
the race?

It couldn't
ketchup.

What do you put in a barrel
to make it lighter?

A hole.

What did the one sock
say to the other sock
in the dryer?

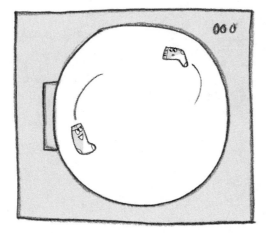

"See you next time round."

Why did the bug look away?

Because the centipede.

Why did the scientist remove the bell from her front door?

Because she wanted to win the no-bell prize.

What do you get when you cross a dinosaur with a pig?

Jurassic Pork.

Why did the watch go on vacation?

He wanted to unwind.

How do you make a witch itch?

Scratch
Scratch

You take away the W.

Why are riddles like pencils?

They're useless unless they've got a point.

Did you hear about the angry pancake?

It just flipped.

What do hedgehogs say when they kiss?

"Ouch!"

Who made the
fish's wishes
come true?

Its fairy codmother.

Where are cars most likely
to get punctures?

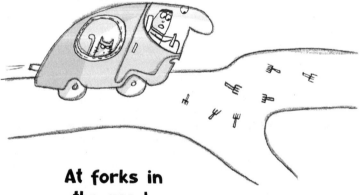

At forks in
the road.

What did the one eye say to
the other?

"Between you and me,
something smells."

Where do ghosts
mail their letters?

At the ghost
office.

What do you call a fish with no eye?

Fsh.

What name did the snail give to her shell?

Michelle.

What did the zero say to the eight?

"Nice belt."

What is a shark's favorite game?

Swallow the leader.

What did the one volcano say to the other?

"I lava you."

What do ants take when they're ill?

Ant-ibiotics.

Where do animals go when their tails fall off?

To the re-tail store.

What is a pig's favorite ballet?

Swine lake.

What has ears like a
cat, a tail like a cat,
but is not a cat?

A kitten.

What's pink and
fluffy?

Pink fluff.

What's blue and
fluffy?

Cold pink fluff.

What's the highlight of a cannibal wedding?

Toasting the happy couple!

What happened to the cat after it ate the clown fish?

It felt funny.

What belongs to you but others use more?

Hi, Steve.

Your name.

Don't trust stairs!

They're always up to something.

What's worse
than a worm in
your apple?

Half a worm
in your apple!

What do you get when you cross
a ghost and a cat?

A scaredy cat.

Why are dogs such weird dancers?

Because they have two left feet.

What goes ha, ha, ha, ha, ha plonk?

A skeleton laughing its head off.

What can you
carry even though it
weighs over
150 pounds?

A scale.

What's gray but turns red?

An embarrassed elephant.

When does the moon burp?

When it's full.

When is it bad luck to be followed by a black cat?

When you're a mouse.

Why should you always take a pencil to bed?

To draw the curtains.

What has 4 legs and goes, "Oom, oom"?

A backward cow.

Why was the rake
so excited about
the future?

Because it was
about to turn over
a new leaf.

Where do letters sleep?

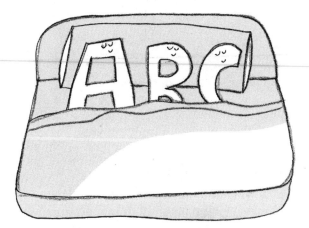

In an alpha-bed.

Why is it so hard to fool a snake?

Because you can't pull its leg.

skritch
skritch

Why was the sheep itchy?

Because it had fleece.

What does 234y3x +
334y/547z x 0.021(0.44) /
y²99 and z - 63/22 get you?

A headache.

What do you call
a bird that's been
eaten by a cat?

A swallow.

Why did the crab
never share?

Because he was
shellfish.

What happened to the dalmation that fell into the washing machine?

It came out spotless.

What did the rope say after it got tangled?

"Oh no, knot again!"

I entered a joke-writing competition ten times and hoped I'd win.

Sadly, no pun in ten did.

Why did the lady divorce the grape?

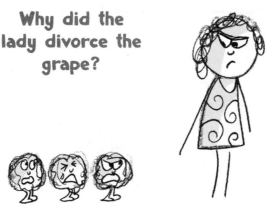

Because she was tired of raisin' kids.

What did the one ghost ask the other?

"Do you believe in humans?"

How did the man cut the sea in half?

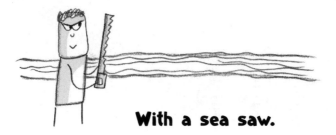

With a sea saw.

What happened to the monster that swallowed an electricity generator?

It was in shock for a month.

Where do birds invest their savings?

In the stork market.

How does a mouse feel just after it's taken a shower?

Squeaky clean.

Why did the cannibal eat his mother's sister?

Because he was an aunt-eater.

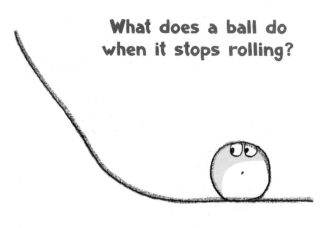

What does a ball do when it stops rolling?

Looks round.

Why are frogs
so happy?

Because they just eat
whatever bugs them.

What's the difference between a
greyhound and a duck.

One goes quick and the other
goes quack.

What is the longest word?

SMILES.

Because it has a mile between the first and last letters.

When do elephants have eight legs?

When there are two elephants.

What runs but doesn't get anywhere?

A fridge.

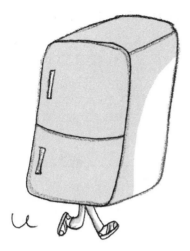

What do cows like to dance to?

Any kind of moosic.

Why do birds fly south for the winter?

It's easier than walking.

Why do pandas like old movies?

Because they're black and white.

What do witches race on?

Vroom sticks.

How do you prepare for an astronaut's birthday?

Planet.

What does a cat say when you step on its tail?

"Me-ow!"

What did the tie
say to the hat?

"You go on ahead.
I'll hang around."

Why can you never trust atoms?

Because they
make up
everything.

WOULD YOU RATHER...

Sleep in a Bed?

beep
beep

beep

... or
Beep in a Sled?

What do you call an overweight dog?

A round hound.

What kind of ant is good with numbers?

An account-ant.

I'm reading a book about anti-gravity.

It's impossible to put down.

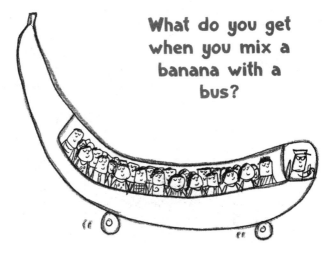

What do you get when you mix a banana with a bus?

A fruit that can seat 36 people.

What's the noisiest sport?

Tennis, because there's always a racket on the court.

Why did Cyclops have to close his school?

He only had one pupil.

When is a car not a car?

When it turns into a garage.

Did you see that film about beavers?

Best dam show I've ever seen.

How do cats eat spaghetti?

With their mouths, just like everyone else.

Why do the French eat snails?

They don't like fast food.

What is a French cat's
favorite dessert?

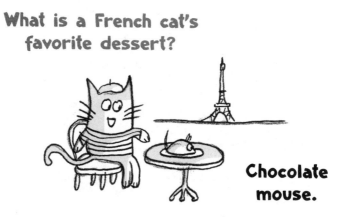

**Chocolate
mouse.**

What do you call a sad
strawberry?

A blueberry.

What is the loudest
kind of pet?

A trumpet.

On what day
of the week do
chickens hide?

Fry-day.

What do you get if you cross
some ants with some ticks?

All kinds
of crazy
antics.

Why did the nurse go to art school?

To learn to draw blood.

How do you get straight As?

Use a ruler.

What do you get when you whisk milk, butter, sugar, and 100 eggs?

A very sore arm.

How can you tell an elephant from a mouse?

**Try lifting it.
If you can't, it's an elephant.**

What do you call a donkey with 3 legs?

A wonky.

What's the difference between legal and illegal?

One's a sick bird.

What sport do you play with a wombat?

Wom.

Did you hear about the guy who invented Lifesavers?

They say he made a mint.

Who built King Arthur's
round table?

Sir Cumference.

My mom bet me $100 I couldn't
make a car from spaghetti.

**You should have seen
the look on her face
as I drove pasta.**

What's red and goes up and down?

A tomato in an elevator.

Why did the orange stop?

Because it ran out of juice.

What shoes are made from banana peels?

Slippers.

What is the best way to catch a fish?

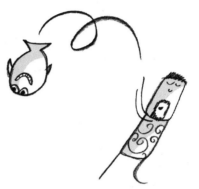

Ask someone to throw it to you.

Where do ants go for dinner?

To the restaur-ant.

What happened after the cat ate a ball of wool?

She had mittens.

What do you call a factory that sells good products?

A satisfactory.

Why was the piano
on the porch?

**Because it couldn't
find its keys.**

I just heard
a joke about a
piece of paper.

It was tearable.

What do cows
love to drink?

Smooooothies.

Where do you find an
upside-down tortoise?

Right where
you left it.

How did Thomas Edison
invent the light bulb?

He got a bright idea.

How did the aardvarks cross the ocean?

In the aard-ark.

When do three elephants under one umbrella NOT get wet?

When it's not raining.

How did the octopus propose
to his girlfriend?

"Can I have your hand,
hand, hand, hand,
hand, hand, hand, and
hand in marriage?"

Why did the mushroom
go to the party?

Because he was
a fungi.

What do you call a banana that loves to dance?

A banana shake.

What fruit is square and green?

A lemon in disguise.

What school subject is the fruitiest?

History, because it's full of dates.

What did the bored cow say when she woke up?

"Oh, just an udder day."

What did the one cat say to the other?

"Have you heard the mews today?"

Why would you throw butter out of the window?

To see a butterfly.

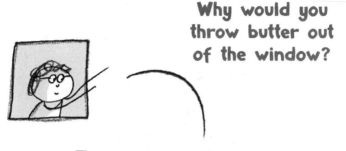

What's the problem with twin witches?

You never know which witch is which.

Why don't witches get sunburned?

They wear suntan potion.

What do you call a man who floats on the sea?

Bob.

What did the farmer use to repair his shirt?

A cabbage patch.

What's the best thing to put in a chocolate bar?

Your teeth.

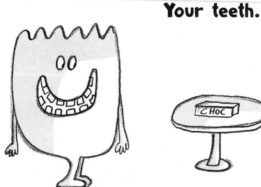

What's easy to get into but hard to get out of?

Trouble.

Why do hummingbirds hum?

They don't know the words.

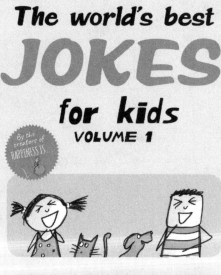

The World's Best Jokes for Kids Volume 2

Andrews McMeel Publishing
a division of Andrews McMeel Universal
1130 Walnut Street, Kansas City, Missouri 64106

www.andrewsmcmeel.com

19 20 21 22 23 RR4 10 9 8 7 6 5 4 3 2 1

ISBN: 978-1-4494-9799-6

Library of Congress Control Number: 201895722

Made by:
LSC Communications
2347 Kratzer Road
Harrisonburg, VA 22802-1004
1st printing—October 15, 2018

For lots more funny, silly, and random jokes,
visit us online:
www.lastlemon.com/silliness
www.instagram.com/silliness.is
www.facebook.com/silliness.is

Send us a joke. If we like it,
we'll illustrate it:
www.lastlemon.com/silliness/submit

ATTENTION: SCHOOLS AND BUSINESSES

Andrews McMeel books are available at quantity discounts with
bulk purchase for educational, business, or sales promotional use.
For information, please e-mail the Andrews McMeel Publishing
Special Sales Department: specialsales@amuniversal.com